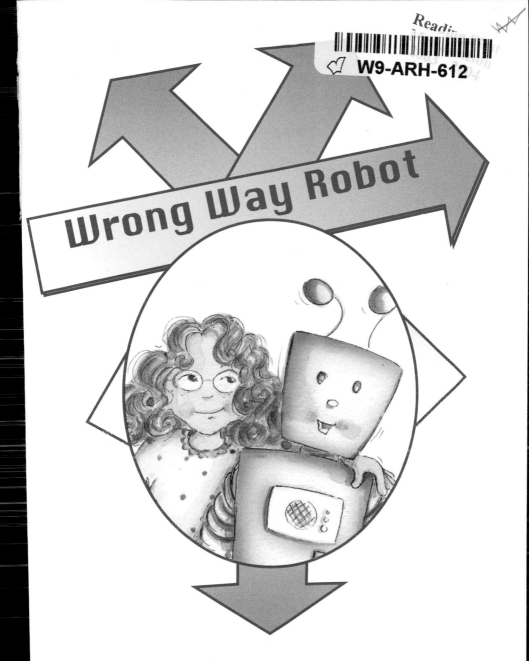

Wrong Way Robot

By Jane Vecchio

Illustrated by Marisol Sarrazin

Modern Curriculum Press

Credits

Illustrations Marisol Sarrizan

Computer colorizations by Jacki Hasko

Cover and book design by Denise Ingrassia

Copyright © 2000 by Pearson Education, Inc., publishing as Modern Curriculum Press, an imprint of Pearson Learning Group. 299 Jefferson Road, Parsippany, NJ 07054. No part of this book may be reproduced or transmitted in any form or by any means, electronic, or mechanical, including photocopying, recording, or by any information storage and retrieval system, without permission in writing from the publisher. For information regarding permission(s), write to Rights and Permissions Department. This edition is published simultaneously in Canada by Pearson Education Canada.

ISBN 0-7652-1377-X

Printed in the United States of America

5 6 7 8 9 10   08 07 06 05 04 03 02 01

1-800-321-3106
www.pearsonlearning.com

Contents

Chapter 1

The B Street Notes . . . . page 5

Chapter 2

Top-Secret Plans . . . . page 11

Chapter 3

Bump! Clank! . . . . page 15

Chapter 4

Robots Everywhere . . . . page 20

Chapter 5

Wrong Way Robot . . . . page 26

Chapter 6

One More Try! . . . . page 32

Chapter 7

Plato Goes to School . . . . page 40

Glossary . . . . page 48

For my mother, with love

The B Street Notes

"Ring! Ring!" The school bell rang. It was Friday at 3:00. The B Street kids were getting ready to go home.

"Hey!" said Lisa. She pulled a tube from her desk. It was a piece of rolled-up paper. "What is this?" she asked.

"I have one, too," said Zack. He held up another paper. "This was in my coat!"

Andy's foot waved in the air. On the end of his foot was a third paper. "Look what I found in my boot!"

Lisa, Zack, and Andy unrolled their papers. On the inside they found a note. They all read: "Saturday at 11:00, meet at Bailey's Store on the corner of B Street. Bring the things on this list with you. Don't tell anyone. This is top secret!"

Lisa said, "My list says to bring my old roller skates."

Zack said, "I need to bring two old balls. What does your note say, Andy?"

"I need to bring some glue, some tape, a ruler, and my paint set," Andy said.

The three kids looked at their notes. Then they looked at each other.

"It's a B Street mystery!" said Lisa.

As the kids walked home, they talked more about the notes.

"Where is Katy?" asked Andy. "I wonder if she got a rolled-up note."

"Yes, where IS Katy?" asked Zack. "I think these notes came from her. She must be planning something again."

Top-Secret Plans

On Saturday at 11:00, Lisa, Andy, and Zack met by Bailey's Store. They stood on the sidewalk and looked around. They didn't see anyone or anything.

"Well, what now?" asked Lisa.

The kids waited. Nothing happened. Lisa walked around the corner.

Suddenly she said, "I've found another note!" Lisa pulled the paper off the store window where it had been taped. "The note says to go to Katy's house," Lisa read.

"I knew it!" said Zack.

The kids ran down B Street to Katy's house.

Zack raised his hand to push the doorbell. Katy opened the door at the same time.

"Come up to my secret lab!" she said.

They all followed Katy to her room.

"What's a lab?" asked Zack as they went up the stairs.

"It's a place where people make and learn about new things," said Katy. "And THIS is what I am making!"

Katy untied a sheet from a big thing in the middle of the room. The thing was a . . .

What was it?

Bump! Clank!

Nobody said a word. Zack's mouth was wide open. Then all the kids began talking at once.

"What is it?" Zack asked.

"It looks like a vacuum cleaner," Andy said.

"Show us how it works!" Lisa said.

Katy said, "This is a robot. I plan to use the things you brought to finish him. I'll show you how he works."

Katy pushed a button on the robot.

The robot began to make a very loud noise. It sounded like BOOM, BUMP!

The robot began to jump. Then suddenly there was a loud CLANK and a grinding noise. The robot stopped.

Katy's mom looked into the room.
"Is everything all right?" she asked.

"Yes, but the robot still isn't working right," Katy said.

Katy's mom looked around. "Maybe you should wait until your dad gets home. He can help you with that robot," she said.

"It's OK, Mom," Katy said. "We just have to put it back together."

"Let's go back to the drawing board," said Katy after her mother left.

"What does that mean?" asked Zack.

"Plans are drawn on a drawing board. It means I have to start over again," said Katy. "Do you want to help?"

"Oh, yes!" they all said.

Chapter 4

Robots Everywhere

The kids worked hard on the robot. As they tried to put it back together, they talked. They wondered what the robot could do.

"I want my robot to do something useful," Katy said, "but I don't have any good ideas."

Later that week in school, the kids'
teacher had a surprise. It made Katy
very happy.

"Class, we are going on a trip to the
Lakeland Science Museum. We can get ideas
for our class science fair," Mrs. Rivers said.

The Lakeland Science Museum was big. Visitors could learn about the weather and about outer space. They could also learn about animals, oceans, and motors.

There was even a room all about robots!
That was the first place that Katy wanted
to see.

Katy saw robots that helped workers make cars. Some robots helped doctors in hospitals. Other robots picked things up under water. Each robot had a useful job.

The rest of the class and Mrs. Rivers finally found Katy. She was still in the Robot Room.

"My robot needs a job to do," said Katy. "Most robots do things people don't want to do or things that are hard."

"Sometimes I don't want to clean my
room at home," said Andy.

"I don't like to set the table," said Zack.

"I get tired of taking out the trash,"
said Lisa.

"That's it!" said Katy. "Let's go back to
the drawing board!"

Chapter 5

Wrong Way Robot

One week later, the B Street kids were in Katy's secret lab. In the middle of the room was something under a white sheet.

"Meet Plato!" cried Katy. She pulled off the sheet.

"Wow!" said Andy.

Katy smiled. She said, "You helped put Plato together. I finally saw how to make him work."

"What can Plato do?" asked Zack.

"He can do all the things I don't want to do," said Katy. "Watch."

Katy held up a small control box. It looked like a remote control from a TV. She pushed a button.

"Watch Plato fold clothes," she said.

Plato rolled to Katy's bed. On the bed was a pile of clothes. Plato picked up a sock. He threw it at the wall.

Then Plato grabbed all the clothes. He threw them all over the room!

When Plato stopped, Katy said, "Well, that wasn't right, Plato. I said fold, not unfold."

Plato said, "Beep."

The kids all laughed.

"Let's try picking up some trash," said Katy.

29

Katy pushed another button. Plato picked up a small trash can.

"Beep," said Plato. He reached into the trash can and took out a juice box. He put it on the floor.

"No!" said Katy. "Put the trash IN the can." She pushed another button. Plato took more trash out of the can and put it on the floor.

Katy told Plato to stop. He went faster. She tried to get him to turn right. He turned left. She told him to be quiet. He said, "BEEP, BEEP, BEEP."

"Plato, you are a wrong way robot," said Andy.

"Beep!" said Plato.

Katy said, "Back to the . . ." and the kids yelled, "DRAWING BOARD!"

One More Try!

For the rest of the afternoon, Katy cleaned her room. She picked up clothes and other things that Plato had tossed around. Later, she went to talk to her dad.

"Plato was doing my jobs for me," said
Katy. "Now I am doing them over."

"Maybe Plato needs a different job," said
Katy's dad.

"You're right," said Katy.

Katy decided to fix Plato for the school science fair. She worked on the robot every day.

Her friends were also working on the science fair. Andy did a report on lizards, like his pet iguana, Lucky. Lisa studied why some balls bounce higher than others. Zack wrote about plants.

A week later, Katy said to her friends, "I think Plato is ready to go again. Come over later and see."

That afternoon, Katy's mother and father and the B Street kids sat in Katy's living room. They waited to see the new Plato.

When they saw Plato, they clapped. Plato looked different. He was wearing a hat and a vest. His arms had many little hands. He was holding a pen, a pencil, a ruler, and other school things.

Katy said, "Plato, hand me the pencil."
She pushed a button. Plato handed Katy
the pencil.

Katy said, "Plato, please hold my book."
Plato did.

"Great!" said everyone.

Katy said, "Plato is ready for school, but there is one little problem. I can't fix it. If I push this button, Plato says, BEEP. Then he acts like a wrong way robot again. Do you want to see?"

"NO!" said everybody.

Plato Goes to School

The next day was the science fair. Katy took Plato to school in a big box. Her dad helped her carry the box to her classroom. The box was closed so nobody could see the robot.

One by one the students told the class about their projects. All the projects were great. Everyone clapped.

Then it was Katy's turn. She opened the box and unpacked Plato. Then she took out her control box.

"This is my robot, Plato," said Katy. "I made him with help and good ideas from my friends."

Katy pushed a button. Plato gave her a crayon. She pushed another button. Plato took a piece of paper from Katy.

"Can I try?" asked Mrs. Rivers.

Katy said, "Sure!"

Mrs. Rivers took the control box.

Mrs. Rivers pulled the stick. Plato put everything he was holding on a shelf. Then Mrs. Rivers pushed the wrong button.

Katy said, "Oh, no!" but it was too late.

Plato said, "BEEP!" He went to Katy's desk. He picked up the papers on Katy's desk and threw them in the air.

"Oh, my!" said Mrs. Rivers. She pushed some more buttons.

Things got worse. Plato closed all the
open windows. He opened the closed
hamster cage. He went to the coat closet.
Then he unhooked all the coats from the
hooks. He dropped them on the floor.
Everyone started laughing, even Mrs.
Rivers and Katy.

At last, Plato went up to Katy. He said "Beep" in a very nice, quiet way. Then he stopped moving.

Mrs. Rivers said, "Well, Katy, this robot is interesting, but not very well behaved." She laughed some more.

Katy patted Plato on the head and smiled.

"Plato is my wrong way robot some of the time," said Katy. "Soon he will be a right way robot all of the time. I just have to go back to the drawing board!" The B Street kids cheered.

Glossary

grinding [GRYN dihng] rubbing or pressing in a noisy way

lab [lab] a laboratory; a room or building where science work is done

museum [myoo ZEE um] a building for keeping and showing important things from art, history, or science

mystery [MIS tur ee] something unknown

project [PRAH jukt] a plan for making or doing something over time

remote control [ree MOHT kun TROHL] a small, flat box with buttons on it that can be used to direct a toy to move

robot [ROH baht] a machine that can do things people do

vacuum cleaner [VAK yoom CLEE nur] a machine that cleans rugs and floors by sucking up the dirt